Two Travelers and a Bear

An Aesop Fable

Retold by Carmel Reilly

Illustrated by Celeste Goulding

Chapter 1

Walking Through the Forest

One day a traveler and his friend were walking from one town to another. As they went along, the friend said, "Why don't we take a shortcut through the forest? It will be much quicker than walking along this road."

The traveler replied, "I'm not sure. I've heard that the forest is a dangerous place. There might be wild animals."

His friend laughed, "Don't be afraid. We'll be all right."

After they had been walking for a few minutes, they found themselves deep in the forest. It was quite dark. They couldn't see very well, but they could hear strange noises.

"I feel frightened," said the traveler.

"There is nothing to worry about," said his friend. "It's just the wind in the trees."

As they walked on, the noises became louder, and the traveler started to shake.

"I really am scared," he said. "I'm sure I can hear a bear."

A Large, Dark Shape

Just then there was a loud, fierce growl.

The traveler and his friend stopped and looked at each other. Now they were both frightened. The traveler grabbed his friend by the arm, but his friend shook himself free and started to run. He ran deeper into the forest and quickly climbed a tree, leaving the traveler standing alone on the path.

The traveler was so scared he couldn't move. In the distance he could see a large, dark shape moving toward him.

The traveler wished his friend had not run away because now he had no one to help him. He knew he had to think of something quickly. It was too late for him to run and hide, so he decided to play dead. He fell to the ground, closed his eyes, and lay very still.

For a few minutes everything was quiet, and the traveler thought the bear must have gone past him. Then he heard a loud thud and a deep growl, and he knew that the bear was right beside him.

The traveler heard the bear walk slowly around him and then stop. He began to feel sick. He wondered what the bear was going to do.

The traveler could feel the bear's hot breath on the back of his head, and he could feel the bear's wet nose on the side of his face. He felt sure that the bear was going to eat him.

Chapter 3

Friendship

The bear sniffed around the traveler for a few minutes. Then just as suddenly as he appeared, the bear turned and disappeared into the forest. The traveler lay very still for a long time. He was very scared.

He waited until he knew that the bear had gone.
Then he sat up and called to his friend.

"You can come out now," he said.

The friend scrambled down from the tree and walked back to the path. The traveler was very angry.

"Why didn't you help me?" he yelled.

"I'm sorry," said his friend. "I was afraid."

Then a minute later he said, "When I looked down from the tree, I could see the bear bending over you. It looked like he was whispering something in your ear. Did he say something to you?"

The traveler looked up at his friend and began to laugh. He laughed so much that tears ran down his face.

At last he stopped and said, "Yes, the bear did tell me something."

"He did?" said his friend.

"Yes," replied the traveler as he got up off the ground. "The bear told me that good friends look out for each other. He said a real friend would never have left me to face a bear by myself. And I think he was right. Don't you?"